Thank You,
Amelia Bedelia

Thank You, Amelia Bedelia

Story by Peggy Parish

Pictures by Barbara Siebel Thomas

based on the original drawings by Fritz Siebel

SCHOLASTIC INC.

New York   Toronto   London   Auckland   Sydney
Mexico City   New Delhi   Hong Kong   Buenos Aires

All rights reserved. Published by Scholastic Inc., 557 Broadway, New York, NY 10012, by arrangement with HarperCollins Publishers. SCHOLASTIC and associated logos are trademarks and/or registered trademarks of Scholastic Inc.

ISBN 0-439-45493-X

12 11 10 9 8 7 6 5 4 3 2 1   3 4 5 6 7 8/0

Printed in the U.S.A.

For Ann, Jack, and Brad Rost

Mrs. Rogers was all in a dither.

"Great-Aunt Myra

is coming today."

"Now, that is nice,"

said Amelia Bedelia.

"I do love company."

"We've been trying for years
to get her to visit,"
said Mrs. Rogers,
"but Great-Aunt Myra says
the only place she feels at home
is at home.
So everything must be exactly right.
We do want her to be happy here."
"Now don't you worry your head,"
said Amelia Bedelia.
"I'll fix everything.
What should I do first?"

"Well, the guest room
must be made ready.
Strip the sheets off the bed.
Remake it
with the new rosebud sheets,"
said Mrs. Rogers.
"Thank goodness you're here."

Amelia Bedelia went

to the guest room.

"These folks do have odd ways.

Imagine stripping sheets

after you use them."

Amelia Bedelia shook her head.

But she stripped those sheets.

Amelia Bedelia had just finished
when the doorbell rang.
"That must be the laundryman
with Mr. Rogers's shirts,"
called Mrs. Rogers.
"Please check them
and make sure
they're all there."
Amelia Bedelia hurried to the door
and took the package.

15

Amelia Bedelia opened the package.

She unfolded each shirt.

"Two sleeves, one collar,

one pocket, and six buttons.

Yes, they're all here."

"There's not a thing missing,"
said Amelia Bedelia.
"Now to check them.
It would be a sight easier
to buy them already checked,"
said Amelia Bedelia.
But she quickly checked each shirt.

Mrs. Rogers

came downstairs in a rush.

"Amelia Bedelia,

my bright pink dress

has spots in it.

Please remove them

with this spot remover.

Leave the dress out.

I will wear it tonight.

Now I must go to the market."

Amelia Bedelia looked

at the bright pink dress.

"I don't see any spots.

This dress just needs washing."

Then another dress

caught Amelia Bedelia's eye.

"She must have meant

her light pink dress.

Now that one sure is spotted."

Amelia Bedelia held the dress up.

"It looks mighty nice

with the spots in it.

But I guess

she's tired of it that way."

Amelia Bedelia put spot remover
on each spot.

Then she waited.

Nothing happened.

"Didn't think

that stuff would work,"

said Amelia Bedelia.

She got the scissors.

And Amelia Bedelia

removed every spot from that dress.

"Amelia Bedelia,"

called Mrs. Rogers.

"Please take these groceries."

Amelia Bedelia ran

to take the bag.

"Here are some roses, too.

Do scatter them

around the living room.

I must get my hair done now.

While I'm gone,

wash all the vegetables

and string the beans.

If you have time,

make a jelly roll.

Great-Aunt Myra

does love jelly roll,"

said Mrs. Rogers.

Amelia Bedelia stopped
in the living room.
"Seems like roses would look nicer
sitting proper-like in vases.
But if she wants them scattered,
scattered they will be."

Amelia Bedelia went on

to the kitchen with the groceries.

She washed all the vegetables.

Then she found a ball of string.

And Amelia Bedelia

strung all those beans.

"Jelly! Roll!"

exclaimed Amelia Bedelia.

"I never heard tell

of jelly rolling."

But Amelia Bedelia

got out a jar of jelly.

Amelia Bedelia tried

again and again.

But she just could not get

that jelly to roll.

Amelia Bedelia washed her hands.

She got out a mixing bowl.

Amelia Bedelia began to mix

a little of this

and a pinch of that.

36

"Great-Aunt Myra
or no Great-Aunt Myra—
there's not going to be
any rolling jelly
in this house tonight,"
said Amelia Bedelia.

37

Mr. and Mrs. Rogers arrived home

at the same time.

Mrs. Rogers called,

"Amelia Bedelia,

please separate three eggs

and pare the other vegetables

you washed.

I'll do the cooking."

Then she and Mr. Rogers

hurried upstairs to dress.

Amelia Bedelia took out three eggs.
"I wonder why they need
to be separated.
They've been together all day
and nothing happened."
But Amelia Bedelia
separated those eggs.

"Pair the vegetables!"

Amelia Bedelia laughed.

"Here, you two go together—

and you two.

Now be careful,

or I'll be separating you, too."

Amelia Bedelia

went up to Mrs. Rogers's room.

"What should I do

with these stripped sheets?"

she asked.

"Stripped sheets!"

exclaimed Mrs. Rogers.

But she got no further.

Mr. Rogers roared,

"What in thunderation

happened to my shirts?"

"Oh, don't you like big checks?

I didn't have time

to do little ones.

But I will next time,"

promised Amelia Bedelia.

"My dress!" exclaimed Mrs. Rogers.

"It's full of holes."

"Yes, ma'am, I removed

every single spot,"

said Amelia Bedelia.

Before Mrs. Rogers

could say any more,

the doorbell rang.

"Great-Aunt Myra,"

said Mr. and Mrs. Rogers.

They rushed to the front door.

"Good evening, grandniece.

Good evening, grandnephew.

My, that trip made me hungry,"

said Great-Aunt Myra.

"I'll cook dinner right now,"

said Mrs. Rogers.

Everybody went into the kitchen.

"Amelia Bedelia,

did you string the beans?"

asked Mrs. Rogers.

"Yes. See—they do

give such a homey look,"

said Amelia Bedelia.

"Where are the eggs

I asked you to separate?"

said Mrs. Rogers.

"Here's one,

one is behind the clock,

and the other is over there.

Did I separate them

far enough apart?"

asked Amelia Bedelia.

Mrs. Rogers said nothing.

So Amelia Bedelia went on.

"And I paired the vegetables.

They went together real well,

and there weren't any left over."

Mrs. Rogers slapped her hand

on the table.

It hit right in a sticky blob.

"Ugh! What is that?"

she shouted.

"Jelly. I tried to make it roll.

But it just plip-plopped

all over the place,"

said Amelia Bedelia.

"Amelia Bedelia!"

exclaimed Mrs. Rogers.

"How do you get things so mixed up?"

"Things mixed up!

Oh, I plumb forgot,"

said Amelia Bedelia.

She hurried to the stove.

Amelia Bedelia

opened the oven door.

Great-Aunt Myra sat up straight

and sniffed.

"Hot apple pie! I do declare.
Now that's the kind of
mixed-up thing I like."

Great-Aunt Myra announced,

"Grandniece, grandnephew,

I like it here."

"Oh, Great-Aunt Myra,

we're so glad!"

said Mr. and Mrs. Rogers.

They both began to talk at once.

But Great-Aunt Myra

wasn't much for words.

She had her eyes

on that last piece of pie.

Great-Aunt Myra put

the last piece of pie

on her plate.

Then she said,

"Grandniece, grandnephew,

I will visit you often.

That Amelia Bedelia really knows

how to make a body feel at home.

Thank you, Amelia Bedelia."

Amelia Bedelia smiled.

She and Great-Aunt Myra

would get along.